love
A STORY

Stewart St. John & Todd Fisher

love

A STORY

love
A STORY

*

THE ST. JOHN-FISHER COMPANY
©2011 Stewart St. John and Todd Fisher

Book Design by India Redman

ISBN 978-0-9830463-3-2
Library of Congress Control Number: 2011900769

LOVE: A STORY

FIRST PRINTING

The St. John-Fisher™ Company

dedication

To all those who have loved us,
and to all those we have loved...
how blessed are we all.

introduction

In the stillness of life, in the silence of every moment, is an invisible energy that fuels us all. It sustains us. It gives us the strength to go on. It enables us to connect. To express our feelings for one another. To enjoy life. To laugh. To understand. To feel compassion. To forgive.

We call it love.

A simple four letter word that evokes so many different descriptions and responses and feelings. We can be "in love", we can "love unconditionally", we can be loved by another and we can even be confused by love. The myriad ways love affects us, plays with us, dances and delights us, confounds and sometimes even leaves us yearning, is absolutely endless.

Love feeds the heart and soul of every man, woman and child on the planet; without it we would simply cease to be.

Love is Source. God. All That Is. Love is the sweet gaze of a newborn staring back at you. Love is finding your soulmate. Love is letting someone go. Love is honoring Self. Love is gentle. Love is knowing that you've just helped someone do something, buy something, become something that they couldn't on their own. Love is forgiving your enemy. Love is forever. It's that warm feeling that bubbles within.

Sometimes the world seems loveless. The media would have us believe that all the love has been sucked out of the planet, and that we're all living in despair and sadness. But that couldn't be further from the truth. Love is everywhere, and it is eternal.

You just have to Know it's there. Or, more accurately, remember it's there. And always has been. And always will be.

The story and words in this book are meant to reawaken you to the abundant love around you right now.

So settle back and relax, enjoy a warm cup of tea or a hot cup of coffee, cozy up next to a fireplace, take a long walk in the park... do whatever you need to do to get comfortable and open yourself to a deep serenity and awareness of the beauty of life and each other. Because when you love, whether you are flowing it or receiving it, you are realigned with the energy of the Universe ... and you become the magnificence of Who You Truly Are.

Stewart & Todd

love

A STORY

love
is powerful

I don't tell this story very often anymore, even though I find myself living in a world that needs to hear it now more than ever. I learned long ago that the best way to share something as powerful as what happened to me is to let people inquire about it on their own. When someone asks, you see, there is a true desire to receive, as opposed to seeking them out and force feeding them whatever you have to say, no matter how incredible it is or how much it will help.

So I have written it all down, allowing people to find it and decide for themselves. I need not convince anyone,

love

is never lonely

for I know the truth and that's all that really matters.

If you find yourself reading these words then I can only assume you've been asking, maybe on a level you're not even aware of, and you've drawn this story to you the way I attracted the entire experience to me.

I'm still surprised any of it happened at all — given my unremarkable life up until that point. I was born and raised in a small Central California farming town about two hours south of San Francisco. I was the middle child, slightly overweight and, with the

love
is in
all of us

exception of being a short-term member of the Rainbow Girls upon the request of my mother, shied away from groups and clubs, preferring to be alone.

It's not that I didn't like people, I just felt so awkward that I didn't think people would like *me*. I slowly withdrew inside an invisible bubble that separated me from the world even though from the outside I seemed perfectly content and well-integrated with the rest of society.

However, my bubble didn't protect me from my own self-critical thoughts that played endlessly in my head — sometimes so loudly it was as though

love
cultivates
the heart

the words were actually being whispered in my ear. *"You're hands are too big, not feminine at all." "You're too overweight." "Why can't you just be like the other girls?" "Your ideas are too out there." "You'll never amount to anything, so why try?" "Who would want you?"*

I was convinced that God made a huge mistake and had sent me to live someone else's life. This was compounded by a marriage to a man who treated me exactly the way I was feeling inside, moved me to sunny Southern California, and, after his multiple affairs, my umpteen times of forgiving him, finally left me

love
is life

financially destitute and deeper in a pit of self-loathing. Was it any wonder why the next decade of my life was spent dealing with bizarre health problems?

My four beautiful children were the only saving grace over the years, but the thing about having kids and depending on them too much is that one day they will become adults with their own lives and you will be left with yours. There is nothing more frightening, nor more disheartening than the feeling of not being needed.

Nothing.

love

is free

They were the ones to whom I first recounted my story. My oldest son was very logical about the whole thing and had his grounded theories about who *The Woman* was. My daughters, bless them, were skeptical of the whole encounter and avoided the subject altogether. However, I did notice an increase in the amount of Sunday church invites I received from them both following my revelation. My youngest, who had recently discovered Buddhism, was the most open and did not care if it was true or not because he felt the wisdom gleaned from the encounter was

love

is eternity

the only point worth discussing.

Still, the one thing none of them could deny was how much my life had changed afterwards. The string of events following the encounter that afternoon unfolded like a divine cosmic roller coaster that still leaves me breathless and puzzled when I look back.

That story is for another day.

My kids came very close to losing their mother that Spring. But as I told them, sometimes you have to be lost in order to be found. And I will treasure the

love

*is being able
to give up
being right*

memory of the day *she* found me for the rest of my life.

♥

I remember it so clearly. I had reached the end. I was exhausted from what was a sad excuse for life. I was embarrassed by my financial situation, frustrated with health issues and a dependency on prescription medication, and devastated by yet another failed relationship.

This one was particularly hurtful

love

sees equally

because I had allowed him in so deep.

He said all the right things, but yet I

didn't believe them. I kept pushing him,

testing him, probably because I wanted

to see how much he would take before he

finally gave up and proved to me what I

believed: that he never truly loved me.

Love was something that eluded

me no matter how hard I looked for it,

so when he called and told me that he

needed to take a break, I wasn't at all

surprised.

I didn't even cry.

love

motivates your soul

I just sat on the edge of my bed staring at the worn threads of the dirty brown carpet in my little rented room. It was like an eerie calm came over me and in that moment I decided *that was it.*

I wanted out.

I wanted out of life.

love
is like
a warm
breeze

Zuma was just a thirty minute drive from the little bedroom I was renting in a house up in Topanga Canyon, and, having made these mid-day sojourns a million times before, I knew the perfect spot where no one else would be, especially on a weekday afternoon.

During the off-season, the beaches became a playground for locals, and most of them were either at work or secluded up in their homes overlooking the gorgeous view.

I'd never seen the ocean so blue, the sound of the crashing waves so powerful or felt the breeze so warm.

love
the little things

I dug my feet into the sand and played with it between my toes for a bit, then dug back in again. I closed my eyes and tilted my head toward the sun and felt its stinging heat filling my face. The sound of the wind seemed to make my own thoughts play louder and more intensely in my mind.

Maybe I was never to find love in this life. After all, I had read just about every soul-searching, self-affirming book ever written on the subject of love, life and liberty. I'd done countless online courses, seminars, asked questions of gurus, did guided meditation after

love
*is a song
that you sing
in your heart*

meditation but always came away with this unsettling feeling in my stomach.

Listening to music was about the only time I ever came close to feeling connected to anything — that and doing my artwork.

Freelancing in graphic design and painting sometimes filled the void, but I found it more and more difficult to be inspired as time went on.

I could feel that there was something missing in my life and I decided it came down to love. Or lack thereof.

To me, love was a word that

love
is magical

meant so many things, yet nothing tangible. I decided that it was a sham. There was no such thing! It was just a word created by THEM to make people like ME feel worthless.

As I sat there in my disconnected state, contemplating what I was about to do, I hadn't noticed the woman by the shore.

It was as though she appeared out of thin air. There she was, down by the surf, dressed in worn blue jeans, a v-neck black sweater with a white t-shirt underneath and sandals in her hand. Her hair was blowing effortlessly in the wind,

love
is ageless

and I was mystified by the calmness of
her energy that I could feel from even this
far away.

I watched her walk and stop
along the beach, then walk a few more
steps and stop again. I realized there was
something very familiar about her body
movements and I kept hoping she'd turn
and look back at me so I could actually
see her face, but she never did.

As she started off again, I noticed
something fall from her arm, something
shiny because the sun reflected off of it,
catching my eye. She evidently didn't
realize she'd lost her bracelet, or watch,

love
is the
    foundation
of the heart

or whatever it was, because she kept on moving.

I got up and trudged across the sand and over to the object partially buried in the water's edge. It was a charm bracelet filled with little silver dolphins — I ran my fingers over it and felt butterflies take flight in the pit of my stomach.

I looked up to see that she was farther down the beach, approaching the enormous arched rocks gathered at the end of the crescent-shaped expanse.

"Hello?!" I yelled out, but there was no way she could hear me from where I was. As I stood there staring at

love
is an
invisible force

the back of her, I became certain that

I knew her from somewhere. Was she

someone I had met at a party? One of the

servers from the Sunset Restaurant?

Before I could find an answer, I

realized that I was walking toward her. It

was the strangest sensation I'd ever felt,

an impulse so powerful it was as though

I'd left my body and someone else was

now navigating the ship.

love
captivates

I quickened my pace to catch up and was able to get a better view of her. She was about 5'8", slender, and now I could see that her golden brown hair was thick and beautiful as it tossed around in the wind.

"Hello!" I shouted again, as another wave came crashing down on the coast, drowning out my voice.

She never turned, never looked back — just continued to walk toward the rocks in the distance.

love
runs deep

Frustrated, I found myself jogging to catch up until I was finally directly behind her.

"Excuse me," I blurted, completely out of breath, the words feeling like they were coming more from impulse than intention. "This is your bracelet."

As she turned around to face me, nothing in my wildest imagination could've prepared me for the moment that I finally laid eyes upon this woman. It was a moment that would change my life forever.

love

*is a whisper
on the
lips
of life*

I don't know how it was possible,

but I was suddenly staring into the eyes of

someone who looked *exactly like me.*

Indeed, she *was* me.

love
*is a warm fire
that burns in
your heart*

"Thank you, Emily," she said, smiling and reaching for the bracelet.

I just gazed as she slid the little dolphins over her hand until they rested on her wrist. It was like looking into a mirror — but this mirror was reflecting back a retouched version of myself. The wrinkles and creases that were etched deep into my face and around my eyes were hardly noticeable. The worry lines across the forehead were completely gone. And there was a lightness of being that I could feel radiating from within her, drawing me in.

"What's happening?" I asked,

love

*is being
told that
you're loved*

confused. My legs were trembling and my breathing was becoming difficult and shallow.

"I know, it seems crazy," she said.

Crazy didn't begin to describe what I was feeling. "Are you...?" I couldn't finish the words. I felt my mouth drying up.

"Yes, I am. I'm you."

"How? I don't understand?" I felt the wind literally running out of me.

love
is a hug

It was at that moment she placed both hands on my upper arms and looked me straight in the eye. "Emily, I wouldn't be here if I didn't think you could handle it."

I stood staring at her for what seemed an eternity. There were no words to describe the out-of-body experience that I was having as this living, breathing doppelganger looked back at me.

And then she did something that took me by surprise — she drew me into her arms and hugged me.

love
touches

My body was tense. Rigid. Unresponsive. But as she held me, I felt her loving embrace penetrate my core as I relaxed into her arms.

And then I started to cry. Sob, actually. The kind of sobbing that was guttural. It was as though every emotion I'd ever felt and every disappointment I'd ever experienced was pouring through me in an instant.

It's difficult to explain, but I felt myself *releasing*, and whatever I was releasing was being absorbed by this woman... who was me.

love

*combines
two hearts
into one*

"Let it go," she whispered in my ear as I whaled my tears, my entire body shaking. "Let it go."

She held me so gently, yet tightly, so securely that I never wanted her to stop. I couldn't tell you how long we were standing there — it was as though time had stopped and we were the only two people on the planet.

I cried until I had no more tears, and then I finally pulled my head away from her shoulder and looked at her.

love
is being
lovable

"I'm so sorry," I said.

"Why?" She asked.

"Because..." I replied, searching for an answer.

"Don't be silly," she said, pushing the hair back from my face.

"You're so beautiful," I told her, transfixed by her radiant energy.

"Yes, *you* are."

love
allows

I fell silent for a moment, then asked, "How is this happening? What exactly *is* happening...?"

"All things are possible, Em. You believe that, right?"

"I guess."

"You guess?"

"Well..."

"Ah, so all those books you've read, all those meditations you've done...

love

*is a blooming
flower
kissed by dew*

you were just going through the motions,

but not really feeling or believing them?"

"No, it's just..."

"Infinite possibilities, Em."

"Infinite possibilities," I

whispered, more to myself than to her.

"Walk with me," she said.

love
is delicious

She took my hand and we wandered to an outcropping of rocks that were at least seven or eight feet high and connected to the craggy cliffs all around us. There were small paths in between, so we followed one to a dry spot and found a picnic waiting for us.

White china plates filled with fresh fruit and croissants were set on a speckled red and black blanket. There was also a bottle of champagne, two flutes and an ice chest filled with pastries, crab puffs, cheeses and chocolates.

love

is imagination

"My favorite *everything*," I mumbled, stunned to see what she had manifested. It was as though she had been expecting me. We sat across from each other and she reached over for the champagne bottle, removing the foil to the wire cage underneath.

"So. You're me?"

"I'm you."

"From the future?"

"There is no future, Em. There's only Now."

love
is abundance

"Then... ?"

"Stop trying to use your intellect to figure this out. It's impossible."

"Yes, but I... "

"Just go with the flow, Em."

POP! She had expertly worked the cork and the champagne bubbled over, ready to be poured. I held out the flutes and she filled them both.

"I feel like I'm in a dream," I said.

love
is laughter

"Yes, I can imagine you do," she replied, giggling.

"You seem so happy."

"I am," she said, raising her glass in toast. "Here's to happiness."

"Cheers!" I said, and we both took a sip. Champagne had never tasted better. "Tell me something... how did I, I mean *you*, become so happy and healthy?"

"Wanna know my secret?"

love

is trust

"Of course! Are you kidding me?" I said, eagerly. "I've been searching my whole life for the secret."

"It's going to sound really cliché, Em," she said, as she separated food onto two plates. "I learned to love."

"*You learned to love?*"

"That's the secret."

I must admit, I was a little disappointed to hear her claim *that* was the secret.

love
*is the
journey of
two souls
coming together*

"Learn? But, I've always loved..."

"Have you?"

"Yes. My children would be the first to tell you that. I've loved them with all that I am. I've loved the men in my life..."

"Have you loved yourself?"

I didn't reply, I just sat there with my glass of champagne and turned toward the ocean, looking into blue sky.

love
is intelligence

"I love myself," I said defensively, even though I knew my words were completely hollow.

"Then why is this your last day on the planet?" she asked.

I turned sheet white, unable to look back at her. How did she know? How did she know I had become so emotionally bottomed out that I had decided to end my own life?

"You've been doing things for other people for so long that you've

love
is triumphant

neglected the most important person of all, Emily. YOU."

As she spoke the words, I knew they were true.

"You've always felt like an outsider, why?"

"Because I was never good enough."

"By whose standards?"

I couldn't answer.

love
You first

"You've been loving others, doing for others, caring about others since you were a little girl," she began, her voice strong and certain. "Because in the doing of all of that, you hoped to receive the one thing you haven't felt inside — love. But the conundrum is, until you love yourself, you can't receive the love you want from anyone or anything else. *That* is the secret."

It was quiet for a long time, and then I felt my eyes welling up again.

"Tell me what you're feeling."

love
is knowing

"Empty."

"Why?"

"Because you're right. I don't love myself. I don't think I ever have."

"Why?"

"I don't know," I whispered, my voice cracking.

"Do you want me to tell you why?"

love
flows

I nodded my head yes.

"Because it was drummed out of you somewhere along this physical life. Because you were born connected and aware of *Who You Are* and someone older than you felt threatened because of their own lack of love and so they said something — or did something — that made you doubt YOU. They made you feel unworthy of loving you, and whenever the chord of self-love is broken it creates a life-long need to find it — outside of you... when all along it exists within."

love
is a kiss

The sound of the waves breaking against rock echoed around me as I stared through a curtain of salty tears.

"When I began to love myself," she continued, "I remembered *Who I Really Am.* I realized that I am a Divine Being, worthy of loving myself.

Worthy.

Of.

Loving.

My.

Self.

love
lets go

And if I felt worthy of loving me, surely others would see and feel that and would love me too, and if they didn't, why would I care? Because I still loved me.

I STILL LOVED ME

NO MATTER WHAT."

There was a moment of quiet calm, and then she said, "Look at me."

I turned back to her, taking in the beauty of her face, her body, her spirit.

"What do you see?"

love

expands

I studied her intently. I felt her essence. "I see... someone at peace. Someone... truly happy."

"You see *you*. You see the potential for you, *in me*. You see what you ARE if you allow yourself to be. If you only but *LOVE YOURSELF*."

"How?"

"Let me ask you something," she said, a smile crossing her lips. "If I told you I was in a dead-end relationship and terribly unhappy, what would you say?"

love
*is a smile
in your heart*

"I'd tell you to get out of it."

"And yet, you stayed in relationships for years feeling miserable every single day. Why?"

"Because..." my voice trailed off. I couldn't finish the sentence.

"Because you didn't love yourself enough to say, *'I deserve better,'* and walk away. Do you see?"

I did, and I wondered why I didn't see it before. It was like I knew it the

love
*is alignment
with the soul*

whole time, but it was invisible to me.

"The one person you're with forever is YOU," she said, smiling at me so kindly that I felt it fill my heart. "It's time to choose to love yourself the same way you've loved all the others in your life. Give yourself that courtesy and respect and watch your world change forever."

I sat there thinking about my life and how often I had gone out of my way to make other people feel loved, when what I was really wanting was to feel that love myself. I was demanding it from

love
never dies

others, when the person it needed to come from was me. It's no wonder that all those relationships never fulfilled me — they couldn't. It was like trying to fill a bottomless pit over and over and over.

I thought about the power of love and what it really meant. I realized that until I loved myself, accepted myself, adored myself, that I would never truly know *what love is*, or feel its fullness.

STEWART ST.JOHN & TODD FISHER

love
is a gift

"I want you to have this, Emily,"
she said, holding the dolphin charm
bracelet in her hand.

"Thank you," I replied, reluctantly
accepting the gift.

"On the back of each dolphin
are tiny engraved inscriptions," she said,
turning one of them over. It read:

"Love You First"

I smiled at the coincidence.

love
heals

"There are no coincidences, Em," she said, "you know that. It's all orchestrated by the Love of the Universe."

I could sense a restlessness in her voice, a feeling that our encounter was about to come to a close.

"Wear the bracelet and remember this day," she smiled as she got up from the picnic blanket and brushed the sand off her jeans.

"How could I ever forget?"

love
is being
child like

"You'd be surprised how often people do,"
she responded.

I wasn't quite sure what to make of that
remark. "How do you mean?"

"Love is constantly flowing to everyone,"
she said, "in every moment. It's the very
foundation of existence. Of God. The Universe.
All That Is. Yet, so many people are sleepwalking
through life they don't get to experience love, and
sometimes, even if they catch a whiff of it, they
soon forget. They allow outside circumstances
to take them along paths that are better left
unexplored. When you love, unconditionally,

love
unconditionally

the world comes alive and the magic is yours to experience."

"I'll remember," I said.

She stood looking at me for a moment. "Yes, I believe you will, Em. I have to go now."

I didn't want her to leave me. There were still so many things that I wanted to talk to her about. She insisted she had to be on her way, wrapped me in her arms for one final hug, and then slowly let go of my hand as she turned and walked down the beach, disappearing behind a cliff in the distance.

love
transcends
time and space

I didn't fully understand what I had just experienced, but it felt transcendental. Life giving. Mystical. Beyond description.

All I knew was that my life had been dramatically altered that afternoon, on a day that I had planned to be my last on Earth.

I suppose in some ways it was, because an old pattern had died.

love
is the
solution to
the problem

Standing there alone, I longed for her to come back. But as I looked down at the dolphins sparkling on my wrist, I realized she *hadn't* left.

She was me.

I was her.

love
will set
you free

And in that moment I knew that I was worth loving.

And so,

I finally, truly, really loved.

Me.

love
is clarity

epilogue

love
embraces
the truth

It was around midnight on a Wednesday the following year that I received an email from a man in England. I was working on a graphic for a new client when it popped in. What got my attention was that it came to an email address only a handful of people knew. I stopped what I was doing and read the subject line.

"Special delivery for Emily."

Intrigued, I opened it and found a message from "David".

Dear Emily,

I hope this finds you doing well. I know this might sound a bit strange, but I was recently having dinner at the Bentley here in London when

love
is peaceful and serene

*I noticed the stunning painting in the main room.
I asked the owner about it and he said it was done
by you. The reason it took me by surprise, besides
being an absolutely brilliant piece of work, is
because, well, it felt so familiar.*

*You see, until a few months ago I was an
attorney at the Hutchinson firm here in London.
But, for reasons I won't go into now, I left my career
and followed my dream of becoming a full-time
photographer. I've been snapping away like crazy,
and I wanted to show you something in particular.
Please see the attachment. I promise it's nothing
racy, LOL, but truly something intriguing. Mind
you, I took this never having laid eyes on your
amazing work.*

*Coincidence? Something more? Whatever
it is, I've learned to stay open to the possibilities. If
you are ever in London, I do hope you'll join me for
a spot of tea.*

*Buckets of good wishes,
David*

My hand was trembling as I went to view
the attachment on my screen. It was one of the
most beautiful photographs I'd ever seen.

love
is where
you are
right now

An underwater shot of a dolphin, angled up toward the surface of the ocean, the glow of the bright sun shining down upon his magnificent grey frame.

There was no mistaking it. It was an absolute replica of the painting I sold to the restaurant in London — the one David had seen.

The painting had been inspired by my encounter in Malibu. The encounter that revived my life, and taught me to love myself. I stared at the dolphins dangling on my wrist and smiled.

Coincidence? I knew better than that.

I also knew that somehow, some way, David and I were destined to meet.

I suspected he knew the same.

I also felt like there was so much more to his story and that when we *did* connect, we would be bound by a familiar odyssey.

Boy, was I right.

LOVE: A STORY

about the authors

Stewart St. John and Todd Fisher are co-founders of The St. John-Fisher Company which creates and produces books, music, television, film, apps and gift products in-house and across all media platforms. They are also the online pioneers of the first scripted broadband series and creators of the first mobile soap opera for *Sprint*.

Stewart is a composer and member of the National Academy of Recording Arts & Sciences, as well as the award-winning writer/producer of the family feature film *Seventeen Again*, and has written for some of the most popular and beloved children's television series seen around the world.

Todd is a producer and designer whose artistic eye brings immaculate beauty to whatever he's working on. Formerly a Senior Producer at *Disney*, Todd also worked in interactive marketing at *Warner Brothers*. Todd oversees the creation and distribution of every product produced at St. John-Fisher.

Visit the web site at: http://www.stewartstjohnlight.com